Jacob's
SPECIAL GIFT

A Short Story

ANNIE PERALTA

Cover designed by Cariza Bernabe

Inspiring Voices®

Inspiring Voices books may be ordered through
booksellers or by contacting:

Inspiring Voices
1663 Liberty Drive
Bloomington, IN 47403
www.inspiringvoices.com
1 (866) 697-5313

ISBN: 978-1-4624-1072-9 (sc)

Printed in the United States of America.

Inspiring Voices rev. date: 11/17/2014

About the Illustrator

Cariza Bernabe is a graduate of California State University, Northridge, in 2008 with a degree in Bachelor of Arts, major in art. Has excellent ability in illustration, Landscape painting and Graphic design. She is the illustrator of the book *Collection of Inspirational Poems for Young readers* and *Marianne's Christmas Miracle.*

Jacob's Special Gift

Nature's sound of cascading waterfalls, babbling brooks, falling rain and other sounds are all pleasing to hear and listen to it relaxes, soothes and comforts the mind, a blessing to the human spirit.

Harmonious sounds of songs, musical instruments like piano, guitar violin are all enjoyable and gratifying to the ear and what's more it calms the nerves.

Jacob in his own silent world misses all these sounds including the undesirable noises and distracting sounds of nature roaring thunder, lightning and gusty winds.

The sound of laughter, cries, screams, whistle, ticking clocks, telephone rings and dripping water are all absent in his world.

With the lack of sound in his life however, he still enjoys life he is not prone to worry, anxiety and his reactions to every day motions are less.

Jacob a ten year old boy was born with a hearing

defect a congenital deafness. He is deaf but he is not mute. He could not hear but he can speak.

Inexplicably however, Jacob's auditory system works normally only when he hears and identifies voices or sounds coming from people talking anything associated with bad plans to commit crime or intention to inflict harm on others. He can also hear sounds related to any dangerous event that is happening or about to happen.

When he hears bad conversation either far or near, his ear vibrates giving him unexplainable pain a signal he is about to hear voices and sound that something wrong is happening or about to happen in some place, and his auditory nerve works with his brain where to perceive and determine the origin of the sound.

After which he makes an attempt to follow this sound or voices and find ways to stop or prevent anything injurious from occurring.

For any other ordinary conversation or sound he has no way of hearing or comprehending he is merely deaf for which his mother can't simply understand.

Across the street lives Elisha his friend and neighbor a normal girl age nine, can hear see and talk, with golden brown hair medium length, sometimes in cute pony tail if not braided, has adorable laughing brown eyes, glowing skin sweet pretty face. Oftentimes they play at Elisha's backyard lawn it has a wooden swing over a big tree or at times they just play jump rope or catch a flying disc known as Frisbees.

Elisha and Jacob live in a small town called Maple side Creek. It is a mixed community of rich, not so rich and middle income family, strong and sustainable, with small and large banks, coffee shops, restaurants, and other businesses, a small chapel, a Park where Jacob and Elisha walk or ride their bikes. It is an urban community close to farmland and a small river where small boats are docked.

Matt, Elisha's father was very much against Elisha getting close to Jacob. He knew Jacob's defect.

"Elisha I told you not to invite that boy here anymore." One day her dad told her.

"But why dad, we were just playing, he's a nice boy."

Martha, Elisha's mother heard the dad talking and said.

"Matt isn't it preposterous what you just said why not let the kids play?"

"How can you call it play, the boy is not normal he cannot hear."

"But they get along well."

"Yes because Elisha is forced to learn how to use sign language."

"What's wrong with that? It is still a way to communicate."

The father has plans of relocating to another town just for Elisha to be away from Jacob.

"Dad why are you so hard on Jacob is it because he is handicap."

"I grew up here, all my friends are here and I like my school I don't want to leave this place." Elisha continued.

Jacob gave Elisha a dictionary of basic sign language and the sign alphabet so she may learn. Each alphabet is specified by using fingers and palms of the hand. It is used for spelling names and places. He also showed a CD where she can watch two people conversing using the sign while an interpretation is appearing on the screen. Elisha's enthusiasm made her learned fast and with so much fun, now she can communicate with Jacob.

Jacob's family communicates with him through sign language. His father Luke and his mother Esther and his two sisters Abigail age eight and Gracie age five all learned how to use the sign language. Esther have been receiving advice from Jacob's doctor about a surgery or cochlear implants but Esther did not approve of it she is concerned about some risks or complications.

Esther usually stays at home to take care of the three children, Luke is a computer engineer and he has a business partner where they run a computer business on communications and technology.

One day Jacob was with his mom at the small town bank, while Esther was in line to reach for the next bank teller without noticing, Jacob went outside when he experienced vibrations on his ear, and pain then he heard soft voices of two people planning to rob the bank talking about the time of entry and the time to exit. He didn't exactly know where the voices are coming from. He followed where the direction of the voices by walking further in the street and he saw a parked van and inside were three men, he saw the two men whom he heard talking. He went near looking at the men until he was noticed. One of the men got out of the car and so was the other one Jacob sensed that they were after him so he ran fast back to the bank. Esther has just finished with her transaction and was worried when she did not see Jacob she searched inside around the bank then went outside much to her surprise she saw Jacob running while two men were chasing him. When Jacob came to his mom he was so frightened he held her arm tightly.

"Why are you chasing my son?" Esther asked the two men.

"He was eavesdropping listening to our conversation"

"Eavesdropping? " Esther was surprised at what she heard from the two men. "You thought he was eavesdropping so you were chasing him. And what are you going to do with him because he heard what you were talking about? Let me tell you something my son is deaf and whatever it was that you were talking about, and afraid he must have heard he had no idea about it." She answered in high tone.

And Esther used a sign language to ask Jacob "Is it true what they said, that you were listening how did that happened?"

Then Jacob answered in a sign "I want to tell you something later."

When the two men saw that Esther and Jacob were using sign language they just left.

After the men were out in the street, Jacob told her mom by whispering.

"Mom you have to believe me that those men were planning to rob this bank. I heard them." Esther was surprised to hear Jacob speak. Jacob can speak and hear so she stopped using a sign language.

"How did you know that, are you capable of hearing now?

Jacob answered talking "I will tell you when we get home mom. What is more important is for you to inform the manager that there will be a robbery in the bank today."

But Esther was very surprised yet insistent "Jacob you can hear my words now even if I don't use the sign language. Can you hear me now?"

"Yes for now mom, but I can only hear whenever there are some unruly people planning to commit a crime."

"That's strange how do you do that?" Esther is still in disbelief.

"First my right ear vibrates and there is pain, after that I could hear voices then my mind tells me to identify where the voices or the sound is coming from that's how I recognize it. But mom can you please hurry and tell the manager."

"But how are they going to believe us? What if they ask how did you hear? You are deaf."

After she heard what Jacob said she wants to call the police but she decided to let the bank do it.

Although hesitant Esther went inside the bank again and talked to the manager about the exact time the two men are planning to rob the bank, the manager was a little confused upon hearing it came from a deaf boy. He knew Jacob is deaf.

"He is deaf but he can hear a bit." Esther created an excuse just to convince the manager.

"Well it's up to you to believe or not. I think the best thing to do now is to call the police." Then they left and went inside the car.

The manager although was not convinced just called 911 and right after he hung up the robbers already went inside the bank, he still couldn't figure out how a deaf boy could hear these wicked men's conversation, but before robbers could ask for money and harm people, the police immediately arrived and arrested them.

Esther hurriedly drove to leave the bank she couldn't wait for Jacob to tell her everything

When Jacob and Esther reached home she eagerly demanded Jacob for an explanation.

"So how did this come about?"

"Mom, while I was in the bank something vibrated

inside my ear then there was pain then I heard voices only me can hear that something bad was going to happen, my mind made me identified where the sound and voices were coming from, which pressed me to follow and I didn't know why it compelled me to do so, then I saw and heard these men talking about robbing the bank."

"And I can relate to you or to anybody without using a sign language but this takes place only during the occurrence of the incident giving me a chance to describe the people and their wrongdoings. I can hear and talk, but for any other ordinary conversation after the incident I cannot hear anymore."

"So this is only a temporary occurrence." Esther said

"That's it mom"

"That's bizarre" She stammered

Esther has learned that her son's auditory nerve functions normally only on unexpected situation and that made her concerned and bothered.

Although remarkably puzzling for her, knowing her son can hear only on certain occasion she was scared and worried that he will face a number of encounter just like what happened in the bank and she is troubled about the danger he might be involved into.

"Why should this happen to him. What could be the reason for this?" Esther asked herself wondering.

Esther took Jacob to the doctor to be examined.

Esther did not mention anything about the incident and what Jacob is experiencing before he could hear something.

The doctor spoke to him by asking questions without using a sign language.

"Can you talk to me without a hearing device or machine?" The doctor asked.

Jacob just looked at the doctor's lips without saying anything which indicates he did not hear what the doctor was asking.

Esther allowed the doctor to examine further whether he can hear more. The doctor put an ear phone to Jacob's ear and connected it to the machine so he could listen while the machine produces different sounds of nature like birds, waves, winds, breeze on trees but he couldn't hear anything there is nothing that was found in him he is still the same born with hearing defect.

Upon coming home Esther called Luke in his office and mentioned to him what happened to Jacob while they were at the bank, Luke was astounded but also terrified for this might involve Jacob with some people creating trouble or other injurious activities towards others as a result of what he can hear.

"But it is not only about getting involved in it, he was able to help the bank today from being robbed. That stops lawbreakers from committing more crime" She told Luke although she too is very much worried.

Esther dread the sense of his son facing some horrible experiences, she closed her eyes and yield her spirit to the divine power.

"My God why Jacob, he is not yet fully grown."

Then Esther turned to Jacob and talked to him in sign language.

"This is going to be a new experience for you Jacob do you think you are ready to handle it aren't you scared?' Esther asked.

"Scared of what mom?"

"Of hearing only when there is a need to help someone or anybody."

"I don't know mom, what shall I do when I hear that something not right is happening or is going to happen?"

Esther cannot say any word. She doesn't know how she should tell Jacob to ignore what he is hearing and let things to just happen, she feels like her boy has some little mission to fulfill, afterwards, she just said.

"Did you realize you are different from other boys out there?"

"Is it because I am deaf?"

"No, you have a special gift given by God it is true you are deaf but you can hear."

"Only under certain situations mom"

"That's it. Not all deaf individuals can do that. You just have to be careful with that gift not to allow people notice it, that's something you have to treasure may be God has certain purpose for you."

10

Esther has always supplied Jacob while growing with adequate values and beliefs about life and always reminding him not to feel miserable of his handicap. And as a young boy she taught him not to lose faith and hope in God. She gave him strength, optimism and encouragement to accept things the way they are although sometimes he may find it difficult to cope with. Esther also advised him about doubt and faith *"When you have faith, you always see light even during the darkest hours. But when you have doubt you always see darkness even during the lighted hours."* There is always a Bible quotation she reads to Jacob.

Jacob immediately went to see Elisha and told her about his experience and how he heard the two men planning to rob the bank. He told her how his ear vibrates when he is about to hear the voices and sound.

"You mean you can only hear when there are ruthless people planning to perform illegal act or if something wrong is going on or about to turn out?" Elisha asked in sign language sounding very surprise.

"Yes but can you please keep this to yourself only you and my mom know this."

Elisha gave him a nodded yes of assurance.

"What about hearing other sounds like music, laughter, animal sounds and others?" Elisha asked more.

"No, I don't hear any of those."

Suddenly Jacob's ear is beginning to vibrate again which signals there is a sound he is about to hear and that is the sound of an incoming truck screeching on the road about to hit a little girl. His mind identified what he heard and what is going to happen. This girl is going to be run over by the truck so he rushed to the street to find where the sound is coming from.

"Jacob wait!" Elisha shouted.

"Jake, come back here, where are you going?"

He heard Elisha's voice and answered shouting. "A girl is going to be hit by the truck"

Elisha heard Jacob's reply without using any sign language and she answered shouting.

"No don't go there!"

Yet Jacob just continued to run till he reached the road where he heard the sound of the truck coming then he saw the little girl walking home unmindful of the truck coming from behind. Jacob grabbed the unaware girl from her back dragged her fast till both their bodies were cast down into the sidewalk and avoided the incoming truck.

"What are you doing?" The girl yelled asking

"I just saved you from being hit by that truck." He said to her without using any sign language

And they both look into the direction of the truck speeding away.

"That truck was going to hit me?" Said the girl very perplexed.

"Yes."

"How did you know that, how come I did not see you and where did you come from?"

"It's not important where I came from, or if you saw me or not, one thing is for sure you're safe now, next time, don't walk in the middle of the street and be aware of your surroundings."

"Thanks." The girl said.

"You're welcome."

He was about to leave when Elisha just arrived she was gasping for breath for running fast to catch up with Jacob.

"What happened?" Elisha asked in basic sign language as they walked away.

"She's already safe." Jacob said while walking.

"Safe from what"

"She's about to be hit by the truck."

"How did you save her?"

"I grabbed her away."

The little girl was still in disbelief while looking at the two conversing while walking. She was surprised why Elisha was talking to Jacob using a sign language.

"How could he hear me talking if he is deaf?" The girl muttered.

"Who among them is deaf why are they using sign language. Could it be her, but I heard her talking to him." The little girl is still bothered seeing them while Elisha talks to him in sign language and Jacob answers orally. The girl just continued to walk home.

"So you heard a truck's sound and then your mind told you a girl is going to be hit."

"Yes"

"Jacob I don't understand, how can you hear from a distant location."

"Remember what I told you I just hear it."

"Elisha, please only my mom and you know about it don't tell anybody even to your mom you have promised me that already. And today when I saved that girl don't also tell my mom. I don't want her to be worried about me"

"I know but I am still puzzled. Your life might be endangered for what you are doing."

"I can't ignore what I am hearing and it's happening only when someone's life is in danger."

"Jake I'm beginning to be worried about you. Can you stop reacting when you hear any sound or voice?"

"How"

"Just ignore it don't do anything.

"I can't do that Elisha when someone's life is in danger"

Elisha admires Jacob's bravery and concern for helping others but she is also worried about his safety.

Jacob continues to attend school for the deaf. In school he learns lip reading and speech reading. The students have the option to use a text phone mobile, it is only used for texting or receiving text but not for receiving calls they were taught and learned how to communicate by texting. Esther allowed Jacob to carry a text phone.

There is another girl in the class whom he became close with, Angeline, a ten year old girl also deaf at birth. Angeline is a lonely, unsmiling isolated girl, with rosy cheeks, shoulder length golden hair and a lovely face. Jacob tries to communicate with her during break time, Jacob wonders why she seemed not to be mingling with the group somehow he managed to console her and put a smile on her face.

"Cheer up Angeline, did you know that frowning is bad for a pretty face."

One day he brought flowers from her mother's garden and handed them to Angeline.

"For you Angeline"

Angeline was surprised and overjoyed, for the first time there was a smile on her face.

"Thanks, they're beautiful, I appreciate it that was indeed very nice of you."

"How are you doing so far?" Jacob asked communicating in sign language

"I'm doing fine."

"Did you need any help in your work today?"

"No, thanks I'm okay for now."

Jacob is the only classmate whom Angeline wants to communicate with, she can talk slightly, slowly with difficulty and with slurred speech. She is having separate session under a speech therapy.

Jacob would sometimes instill in Angeline's mind the important concept of prayer.

"Don't you feel down and hopeless at times Jacob?" She would ask.

"Down maybe sometimes, I believe it's normal but hopeless no."

"And what do you do?"

"I just pray and it gives me a better feeling after."

"Prayer has great power and it works which means if we have confidence in God and ask anything according to His will He will hear us." He continued.

"Are you still lonesome Angeline. Is something bothering you, is there anything I could do to help?"

"I don't think anybody can help." She said.

"Yes, a silent prayer. Do you believe that whatever prayer is in your heart has already been heard even before they were said?"

Angeline is amazed to find out Jacob's spiritual wisdom. How can a ten year old boy talk about the power of prayer?

One block away from Jacob's house is a small chapel, at the back is where a small beautiful garden enhanced by scented flowers, tropical plants and trees providing sense of comfort for reflection and a quiet place far from the elements of sound. The presence of the cross mounted on the ground with the statue of Jesus heightens the spiritual serenity of the place. Jacob has a devotion to the crucifix.

He faithfully goes there every Friday to offer some fresh flowers he picked up from his mother's garden.

Esther has such a way with flowers. She has a small but well designed garden at their backyard with awesome collection of annual, perennial flowers and plants with amazing colors producing pleasing fragrance, she maintains and keeps the garden growing her favorite varieties of roses, Shasta daisies, lilies, mums, marigold among others, accented by fascinating display of her beautiful orchid collection. Esther believes flowers have magnificent effect to mind and soul.

It is Friday afternoon and as Jacob was walking and getting close to the chapel garden, to his amazement he heard a voice, for the first time he felt no vibration and pain, he heard a live voice talking although no one seems to be around, it is a male voice with deep but low sound which is not typical of any ordinary male voice and speaking slowly saying. *"Come, listen to my words"* He looked further around but he did not see anybody. Then he followed the voice and listened carefully he was taken by surprise when he saw the voice was coming from the statue of the Jesus on the cross, his eyes open talking to him. *"Don't be afraid, Jacob it is me." "Jacob you have a gift and use it only to service anybody in dire need."* The voice continued.

All of a sudden it has stopped talking. Jacob was

speechless. He wanted to ask what gift Jesus was trying to tell. Could it be what his mom told him, a hearing gift?"

He didn't even notice Elisha's abrupt appearance.

"Jacob, I knew I'll find you here, Jacob why are you staring at him?" Asked Elisha in sign language when she noticed he was staring at Jesus in great awe and motion of disbelief. Then Elisha looked at the cross and to Jacob with much surprise.

"Jacob, Jacob, what's going on with you why are you staring at him with wide eyes did something happen?" She asked again.

Jacob still couldn't speak, he doesn't know if he should tell Elisha what he saw and heard or just keep it to himself. What if she does not believe him, then he decided not to. He answered Elisha in sign language.

"No Elisha, nothing, nothing happened."

"Then let's go" Elisha said.

"Okay let's go" Jake answered.

"Are you alright?" Elisha asked again noticing his unusual behavior.

"Yes, I'm fine"

While walking Jacob felt his ear is vibrating again giving him a signal that he will hear voices.

"Jacob is something wrong?"

"I am hearing something"

When Jacob speaks without using a sign language Elisha knew he was hearing voices and sound again.

"What are you hearing again this time?" Elisha asked without using a sign language.

"There is going to be a robbery in the big Jewelry store. I heard the sound of glass being broken."

"Glass, what glass?"

"The top glass of the jewelry display case."

"Where"

"Elisha you have to call the police and tell them there is going to be a robbery at the Bright Star Jewelry.

Elisha and Jacob went to a phone booth and Elisha Called 911 and informed the operator to go to the place Jacob mentioned.

"How did you know all these did you see the robbers entered the store?" The operator answered doubting the voice of a little girl.

"My friend heard about it."

"How did he hear it who's your friend, what's his name?"

"Sorry I can't tell you that." Then she hung up.

"Jake, they don't seem to believe me."

"Then we better go to the jewelry store before it's too late."

"No Jake, we might get harmed there these robbers are armed and dangerous."

But Jacob insisted that they go, the jewelry store is in the town center which is three blocks away from the chapel and they still went and talked to the manager. And because they were kids the manager did not believe them either. But the two kids did not leave they watched the robbers pulled their van. The driver was left in the van. Then they saw an oncoming lady who was about to go inside the jewelry store and Elisha approached her saying.

"Ma'am don't go inside that store there is going to be a robbery."

"What are you talking about?" The lady asked but not sure if she will believe her.

And Elisha pointed the van and in a whispering voice said. "See those three men inside the van, two of them are already putting on their masks and will go inside."

"Oh my God!" The lady said in shocked and terrified tone when she saw the two men put on their masks.

"Can you please call the police because when I called them they didn't want to believe me."

The lady got her cell phone right away went inside her car and dialed 911 and told the operator the place. But the two robbers already went inside and fired two shots upward and shouted.

"Nobody moves this is a robbery!"

"And nobody attempts to go out or you die!" The other man said.

The jewels were strikingly beautiful, precious gems like diamonds, emeralds, rubies, sapphire, pearl set in gold and silver, exquisitely displayed in cases framed with glass on top and all sides. The robbers broke the top glass of the display case and in their bags loaded all what they can get while the other man was pointing the gun to the manager and the customers were in great terror.

Meanwhile outside, Elisha and Jacob were looking for some pointed or sharp object, when they found a nail they carefully hid behind the van, Jacob pricked and punctured one of the back tires letting the air out till it was flattened and slowly unnoticed by the driver they went to the lady's car.

Inside the jewelry store after the robbers' bags have been filled up they rushed to the door and headed to the van, the driver immediately turned the engine but the tire at the back has already been depleted and the van won't move. When the men heard the police's siren they attempted to run but they were entrapped by the police officers and were arrested. The bags of stolen jewelry were taken back and returned to the store manager. "I should have believed those two kids." The manager said to himself.

When Jacob and Elisha saw and heard the police officers, they decided to go out of the lady's car.

"Thanks for your help ma'am we have to go." Elisha said.

In a not too hilly part of the town a mansion is situated up surrounded by majestic old trees and beautifully maintained garden, there is a tall metal gate that opens electronically by a remote, the mansion is owned by Mrs. Eugene, an elderly rich widow woman who lives alone, a servant visits her twice a week. Inside, near the gate is a hidden surveillance camera.

One Saturday afternoon Jacob and Elisha went biking and decided to go a little farther to experience biking in a winding road, they spotted two men stepped out of the parked car by the curb near the mansion, while there was one man left inside presumed to be the driver. They hid in the bougainvilla bush across the street and saw the two men entered inside through the electronic gate using their own remote. The men were thieves. The two kids were wondering how those guys were able to enter the tall metal gate when it is electronically operated. A couple of minutes later the two men came out, seems they were carrying expensive beautiful paintings, when the two men were about to put the paintings inside the trunk of the car, they noticed the two kids, upon knowing they were being watched, they immediately closed the car door and walked towards them. Elisha and Jacob rode in their bikes and pedaled as fast as they could. When the driver saw them going away he followed, even if they were biking so fast Elisha couldn't pedal hard so they choose to leave the bike and just raced on the road till they reached the chapel.

"Let's go inside the chapel." Jacob said.

They tried to get in but the door was locked. They went to the crucifix garden and Jacob talked to Jesus.

"Jesus these men are running after us, they have a gun. Can you please open your eyes and talk again please save us." Jacob said while looking at the cross.

But Jesus did not open his eyes this time. Jacob knew it was because Elisha was with him.

Finally the two men saw Jacob and Elisha in the garden and pointed the gun on them.

"Please don't kill us we will not tell anybody what we saw."

Elisha pleaded in a terrifying voice. But the man won't listen to her pleas and just when the man was about to pull the trigger a violent wind like a whirlwind came about and beat the men's bodies it swept the gun and was thrown away.

"What tha ...." The man was unable to say anything both were being blown by the strong wind.

Much to Jacob's surprise despite the wind blowing hard the trees were calm the flowers were not swayed and the wind was only touching the two men.

This gave Elisha and Jacob the chance to run as fast as they could while the two men were trying to escape from the whipping wind.

When Jacob and Elisha were gone, the howling wind stopped and the man couldn't find his gun. The men's faces were full of dirt almost covered their eyes.

"We have to look for that boy and girl."

"How, we don't even know where they are and

where they live, and it's not safe for us to be hanging around here."

The men just left the chapel garden.

They reached home and Elisha told her mother what happened and how they left their bike on the road. Martha was shocked of what she heard and reported to the police. Elisha was asked to make a description and when the composite image was finished Elisha said.

"That's it, those were the men."

There was an investigation at the mansion, the police turned on the video of the surveillance camera and the faces of the thieves appeared visibly. The old lady was not even aware because she was asleep.

Manhunt went on and the two men were arrested. The paintings were recovered.

One morning in sign language Elisha said.

"Jacob I heard you talking to Jesus while looking at his statue in the garden saying 'Can you please open your eyes and talk to me again.'"

"What did you mean when you said that? Did he talk to you before, did he open his eyes?"

Jacob couldn't answer he's trying to find some words. In sign language he answered.

"Did I say that? Maybe that's my way of asking the Lord for help."

"But you said the word 'again'."

"Maybe he had helped me once and I just want him to do it again."

"What kind of help, you have not mentioned to me anything."

"That was way back" Jacob answered trying to avoid more of Elisha's inquiry.

But Elisha was not convinced she wants Jacob to tell her some more just wondering why Jacob was not telling him everything.

Autumn is under way and starting to reveal its beauty on trees becoming rich in multiple colored leaves and blossoms. Autumn is the season Esther loves most so the family decided to take a short vacation.

The sun is bright, sky clear, and autumn breeze touching the skin like a baby's soft embrace, while on the way Esther enjoys the marvelous views trees and flowers create mostly in highly elevated areas, mountains surrounding the quiet lakeside are peaceful, beautiful huge amount of colorful flowers leaning tenderly on vines and shrubs form like elegant array of precious sparkling tiaras.

Jacob felt his ear vibrating and when Esther noticed him she asked.

"What's going on Jake?"

"Dad, can you turn to the left."

"Why?" Luke asked

"There's a little girl drowning, she's crying for help."

"Where" Luke asked again

"Further down there dad"

Although they do not hear any sound Luke just made a turn to the road Jacob directed, the road is narrow, the place is isolated and inaccessible, alongside is a lake distant from the town and they saw a little girl screaming for help, struggling to make her face stay above the water and almost drowning she doesn't seem like she knows how to swim in less than a minute she will already drown.

Luke pulled the van got out and upon reaching the lake without delay removed his shoes and jumped into the water.

"Be careful dad!" Jacob shouted.

He advanced to swim closer the girl was in the middle of the lake. Luke grabbed her from behind and slowly with full composure they reached the edge of the lake safely. Luke carried the girl. She was exhausted, feeling weak and very cold, shaking and still scared. When they came near the van, first they gave her a towel and immediately a blanket.

The lake doesn't seem to be a popular place for visitors or tourist because of its remote location it is not alive with people.

"How can a little girl come here all by herself" Esther muttered as she saw the girl

"It's okay honey you're safe now." Esther said.

"What happened, how did you get there?" Esther asked her again.

The girl couldn't talk and seemed very frightened.

Abigail opened her bag and offered her t-shirt and jeans. She let her changed at the backseat. Luke went to the trunk and pulled down his luggage took out a towel and changed his wet clothes.

Then Esther asked again. "Don't be afraid to talk so we can help you why are you in this area? This seemed to be a secluded and remote place."

After several minutes of being silent the little girl began to talk.

"What is your name?" Esther asked

"Brittany"

"How old are you?"

"Eight"

"Do you know how to swim?"

"No"

"Where are your parents?"

"I only have a mother."

"So why are you in the lake?"

"My stepfather brought me there and threw me in the water."

"But why"

"I told my mom I saw him with another woman, my mom got mad at him and they had a fight, he knew I was the one who told my mom, he got mad at me, and when my mom left for work he turned to me forced to go with him, I ran but he caught me, put me in his car and drove to this lake."

"We have to go to the police."

"No please, he will kill my mom."

"But this is not right. You could have died there. He will not stop."

Luke called from his cell phone, reached the telephone operator and asked for the nearest police station, the direction to get there from where they are then he drove. He reported to the police the incident and how he rescued the girl from drowning. The police recorded his statement and also the girl's. She was asked to describe her stepfather's appearance and generated from the computer a composite look of her stepfather. Brittany also told them where he works. The police officer notified the nearest police station in the vicinity of his employment as described by Brittany and sent by fax the girl's statement, the composite picture, and issued an arrest order.

The stepfather was resisting when he was being arrested by the police.

"Why are you arresting me" He asked surprisingly.

"For an attempted murder of a little girl by drowning in the lake"

"I don't know what you're talking about"

"Yes you do, we have the statement from the girl."

He was staggered to find out she was alive. Who could have saved her, the place is not even a visitor's place nobody knows where that lake is.

"You will have to testify." The police officer told Brittany.

Brittany got terrified.

"Don't worry we will be with you. We will also testify that we saved you from drowning." Esther reassured Brittany to calm her fear.

The police also called the girl's mother. When her mother saw her daughter and learned what happened she was terrified and hugged her crying.

"How did you catch sight of her?" The mother asked.

"We were on the road on our way for vacation when we heard a voice crying for help so we rerouted to find out where she was and there we saw her in the middle of the lake." This time Luke answered.

"But the lake is too far from the main road how was she heard?" The mother asked.

Esther gave Jacob an expressive look while Luke is talking giving him a signal not to say any word how he heard the girl's voice.

"She was screaming in loud voice." Luke described some more.

"Thank you very much for all your effort in helping to save my daughter. I'm sorry if this has caused you any trouble and disruption on your way."

"Oh no, there's no trouble at all we have saved a life, take care of your daughter" Luke said.

And the mom and daughter stood up to go home.

Brittany thanked Abigail for the t-shirt and jeans she gave her.

Luke resumed driving on to their vacation site till they reached a resort. It is a resort not too crowded very peaceful surrounded with multicolored and vibrant trees, quaint and beautiful lakefront water views very relaxing refreshing and with an essence of privacy, perfect for family traditional vacation to enjoy fishing, boat riding and swimming. Landscape is beautiful with a swimming pool where only tiny voices of little children playing on the water are heard.

There is a picnic area for outdoor dining with tables and built- in grills. Esther prepared some meat and fish to grill.

The cabin is well equipped with just about everything. Lounging chair, air-conditioned and fireplace but Esther preferred to light the fireplace.

After a five day getaway, the family headed back home.

That Friday Jacob went to the chapel garden carrying with him a bunch of new fresh flowers. After Jacob has laid the flowers at the foot of the crucifix he made a sign of the cross and closed his eyes to utter a prayer which he usually does every Friday. When he opened his eyes after praying, he was stunned at what he saw, unexpectedly Jacob saw the figure of crucified Jesus came to life. Jesus was not talking his head was bowed down, his arms stretched out nailed on the wooden cross, he look weak while slowly breathing with difficulty due to excruciating pain, his face full of sweat mingled with blood and Jacob saw the fresh open large deep wound oozing with blood from the skin on the side of his body pierced by the soldiers with their spears and lance during the Roman times. He saw Jesus in his intense agonizing moment his body bathed with blood and fluid.

He only knew about Jesus' sufferings when he read it in the Bible for children with his mother.

But this time Jacob was taken aback couldn't believe at what he is seeing was sorrowfully touched and swiftly tears rolled down his face and said.

"I'm sorry Lord" After he has uttered this he sobbed.

Suddenly Elisha arrived again.

"Jacob..."

When he turned to her she saw his face with tears and asked in sign language.

"Why are you crying?"

"No, no I'm not. Some foreign object just entered my eyes." He answered also in sign language.

"But you were sobbing that is not caused by a foreign object."

"No I was not sobbing" and he wiped off his tears with his

t-shirt and tried to hold back sobbing.

He look again at the crucifix, then Elisha look at it too they were both looking and Jacob saw it now in static position. Jacob realized that the statue of Jesus became alive only to him. Elisha did not see anything. He doesn't know if he has to tell it to Elisha but she may not believe so he decided to keep this experience again to himself.

Still Elisha is in great astonishment. She wants to know why Jacob was in tears.

"Did somebody hurt you?" She asked

"No, no Elisha, nobody hurt me."

"Then why are you crying?"

Still Jacob couldn't talk, and just asked Elisha that they go.

Even when he was already home Jacob still couldn't talk. He cannot forget what he saw in the garden. He cannot even mention it to his mother thinking she will not believe him and might only say "that's impracticable."

"She might also say this time if I have lost my mind" Jacob mumbled to himself.

Or if his mother believes him, Jacob is concerned it might spread all over, then people will pluck to the cross and if the frenzy crowd don't see what they expect and anticipate he might be blamed, he is scared he might be misinterpreted and be branded 'crazy deaf boy'. This gave him a feeling not to talk about it to anyone and decided not to reveal even to his mother about his experience at the crucifix.

Then he asked his mother. "Mom in the Bible why does Jesus love the children"

"Because they are pure innocent believing souls their minds are incorruptible." Esther answered.

The experience he had at the garden gave his life a dramatic significance. His trust enhanced and his faith increased he became much closer to God.

The cold winter air is making its way. Snowflakes are seen slowly and quietly falling like lustrous sparkling crystal beads spreading sheaths on trees and green grass creating a winter spectacular vision.

It is December and two weeks more it will be Christmas. Melodious Christmas songs are dominating the spirit in the air. Poinsettias are in their perfect bloom.

At home Esther, Luke and the children started decorating their Christmas tree with bright alluring flickering lights, they wrapped around the tree and ornately adorned with dozens of shiny balls of different designs and sizes a nativity star is placed on top of the tree. A wreath is hung at the main door.

Luke went up the roof and set out to light up Santa Claus and his reindeer. He also brought out the colored lights and with Jacob's help they both lined the lights along the front walks of the house creating a fantastic array of sparkling lights. They also put strands of outdoor lights above their entrance door.

A nativity scene is set in the front yard, the statue of Mary, Joseph and the baby Jesus in a manger, the Magi, the animals and the Angels, colored lights highlighted the scene. At night all outdoor lights glitter brilliantly.

Esther and Jacob went to shop for toys at the popular toy store in downtown. When they were inside the department store Jacob started to hear a voice of a girl crying and screaming. The store is in the first floor. A distraught man employee who has been fired for breaking company policy and for unethical behavior was planning to commit suicide on top of the building and taking with him a little girl crying.

"Mom, tell the manager to call the police a man is inside this store and will kidnap a little girl to take with him to the ninth floor he will jump with the girl."

"What? Oh Jesus Christ, where is that girl and how can we find her it is too crowded here."

"I don't know mom, I was just hearing the voice."

Suddenly everybody was appalled and disturbed when a man just grabbed a four year old girl while her mother was busy browsing for toys, and run with her to the elevator, waited to get inside, pressed the button going up while the little girl was screaming and crying "Mommy Mommy.. .!"

"There they are mom" Jacob said pointing when he saw the man with the little girl entered the elevator and pressed the door. The door closed before the girl's mother gets closer.

"Hey, bring back my daughter!" The child's mother yelled and she started dialing 911.

"Hello, my daughter has been kidnapped while we were inside this department store. He was taken by a man and he went up the building, please help my daughter." She told the 911 operator.

"It's too late Jake we cannot help." Esther said

"Yes mom we can." Jake answered

"Jake where are you going"

"Upstairs mom"

Hurriedly he entered the elevator and pressed the button going up. Esther followed very nervously and said inside the elevator.

"Jake, you're not serious about this, are you?"

"Yes mom, I am."

"Jake there's nothing more we can do, the man has the girl let the authorities do their job." Trying to convince Jacob not to move up

Jacob was quiet despite Esther's refusal for Jacob to take part on what's going on.

There was a commotion, disturbance and outrage at the department store. The store manager and other staff went out to see the man and also called the police.

Helicopter crews are seen flying surrounding the building.

The rescue team has arrived they're on the ground and made their Life Safety equipment ready in case the suicidal man jumps with the girl. The street became crowded with onlookers emotions are getting high, all eyes fixed upward, creating a suspenseful scenario. There was a media rush, TV vans and reporters with camera men from different stations gathered busy taking videos and covering the event.

The man had already reached the top of the building, some police team are down below watching, waiting if the man will jump.

He was holding the girl still crying hard and very frightened.

When Jacob reached the top the man was already about to get to the edge of the building Jacob slowly walked towards them and told the man in a soft and compelling spirit.

"Mister, please let the girl go don't involve her with your conflict."

"Who are you get out of here would you like to join us too? The man asked in a yelling voice.

"No, please I just want you to let the girl go she has nothing to do with this, look she's so terrified" Jacob was very emotional trying to persuade the man to give up the intention of jumping with the little girl.

Esther felt strained when she heard the man and saw Jacob advanced and said softly and very cautiously.

"Watch out Jake, and don't move any closer"

"Don't come closer anymore or I'll throw her down" the man said in a threatening position.

Jacob stopped moving and talking when he heard what the man said, being careful not to provoke his treacherous attitude, tried to maintain his equanimity but above all the situation made him strung up. He didn't seem to trust the man he'd rather shut his mouth to save the little girl's life from his impending motive, his heart began pounding which made him uncomfortable, he looked down below saw the crowd and realized the loftiness of the building at that point he can't think of any method to use without implicating the girl then he looked up in the sky and uttered a prayer. *"Lord, help me to save this little girl's life. I am not good at scheming what to do right now, it's only you who knows that."*

Of a sudden he saw some officers carrying guns who have reached the top and in quiet hiding. Esther also noticed the armed officers. The little girl still struggling to get out from the man bit his arm hard that made him loosen his grip. "Ouch" the man cried.

The girl got down fast and run shouting "Mommy, Mommy!" Esther interrupted her mildly, although the girl was resisting herself free. Esther stooped down started to stroke her hair gently and wiped off her face full of sweat and tears, pat her back to calm her down.

"That's okay sweetheart don't cry anymore your mommy will be here." Esther whispered to her ear.

The little girl calmed down but still blubbing looking around for her mommy.

The man was about to take the girl back from Esther when the four police officers at once came out from hiding took hold of him from behind, hand cuffed and taken him into custody.

The girl's mother arrived terribly tensed held and hugged her daughter tight. "Oh my baby" And she thanked Esther.

Jacob was in great relief seeing the man taken by the police officers and the girl now with her mother.

"Thank you Lord for helping saved another girl's life." Jacob muttered.

Some reporters and camera men managed to get to the top and started taking pictures and videos. On camera they started reporting the incident.

One lady reporter came close to the mother and the girl started asking questions.

"Can you tell me how your daughter survived this ordeal?"

The mother and daughter did not answer, still terrified while being escorted and protected by one of the police officers trying to evade the camera men and reporters, and led the mother and daughter safely down.

When Esther noticed the reporters were crowding, she and Jacob immediately went down too before they could be asked by the media people why they were there.

Esther was glad this event was over and she placed her arms around Jacob's shoulder and whispered. "Let's do the shopping next time. Let's just go home." At last Esther began breathing normally and peacefully.

Elisha's father works as a construction engineer who is known to be very hard on his workers, he's mean and almost everybody hates him. One day, while at the construction site, two construction workers planned to kill him but they are going to make it look like an accident.

Jacob was at home having some snacks of potato chips when his ear began to vibrate, then he heard the conversation of two workers plotting to kill Elisha's dad by dropping stacks of plywood from the highest level of the building construction. Jacob instantly went to see Elisha knocked at their door and told her what he heard.

"Elisha your dad is about to have an accident today at the construction site"

'How did you know?'

"Didn't I tell you about these voices I'm hearing?"

"Why, what's going to happen to my dad?"

"Two men are going to drop stacks of plywood on him, if you want to help your dad we have to hurry to save him."

"How, we don't even know how to get there.'

Martha just came in from the garden holding basket of flowers and she overheard Elisha and Jacob talking about Matt.

"Did I hear something is about to happen to your dad?"

Elisha was mixed up she didn't know how she would tell her mom without mentioning about Jacob's perception and how she will convince her to believe or agree.

"Oh no mom, but you know what, we have to go to dad's workplace right now." She said calmly.

"Why?" Martha asked surprisingly.

"Something bad might happen to dad today."

"How did you come up with that?"

"I'll explain later, can we please go to the car now he might have an accident that may cost his life." Elisha said her voice starting to rattle while Jacob is just looking at her.

Martha still couldn't believe but she got her jacket, purse and keys and hurriedly they went to the garage.

"Mrs. Muirfield, can you please call my mom first and inform her where we are going because I have not told her we are going to see Elisha's dad." Jacob said

"Why, are you coming with us too?" Martha asked very perplexed.

"Yes mom, he is coming with us." Elisha answered

Martha took her cell phone from her purse and called Esther.

"Esther, Jacob will be with me and Elisha, we are going to see her dad at his workplace."

"What? Why did he not tell me?"

"He was in hurry to see Elisha. I think he told her something about Matt getting into an accident so we have to hurry."

"Oh my God" She mumbled.

Esther became anxious and troubled that this might be one of those voices Jacob must have heard so she asked Martha for the direction in going to Matt's workplace and she too rushed to her car and raced to the construction site of Matt.

She was very alarmed while driving and terrified that something might happen to her boy.

While on the road Martha asked Elisha to call her dad on his cell phone.

"Dad, we're on our way to see you."

Matt was surprised to receive a call from Elisha.

"Why, what's going on?"

"Dad, please listen carefully this is important, you might be in danger so wherever you are now either you are sitting or standing can you move away from that place."

But because of too much noise from machines, tools and other equipment being used by the workers, Matt couldn't understand and hear Elisha clearly.

"Elisha I can't understand you." Then he hung up on her.

"Mom he cannot understand me because of too much noise."

Martha became worried and anxious she drove a little faster but with care.

When they reached the site they don't know where to find Matt, it is a multi complex structural building under construction. Jacob stepped out of the car hurriedly to follow the voice he is hearing and ran a little faster.

"Jake, wait for us!" Elisha shouted.

Jacob made few right and left turns while Elisha and Martha were following him. All around every where is crowded with busy workers engaged in all kinds of work. Jacob spotted Matt standing and giving instructions to one of the supervisors while pointing at the blueprints.

"Mr. Muirfield, please lookout!" Jacob cried out.

When Elisha saw her dad she shouted.

"Dad, get out of that place, hurry!"

"Dad, watch out above you, look!" Elisha pointed above.

The stacks of plywood were already being dropped by the two men on its way about to land on Matt's head. Matt was surprised to see and hear Elisha and Jacob and as he look above he saw the stacks of plywood underway and he immediately moved away from the spot. All workers were stunned and they stopped working. One of the crews below identified the two men who intentionally dropped the plywood, when the two men noticed they were being suspected and their plan failed, immediately they made their way to escape through the pole exit used only in case of emergency. They jumped off the ground and tried to run fast, Martha dialed 911 on her phone, at once Matt using his small megaphone ordered some workers to block the two men, they ran after them, the two men resisted and fought but they were knocked over.

Esther arrived and saw her boy. She walked him a little distant from Matt.

"What's happening Jacob, why did you go here?" She whispered.

"Mr. Muirfield was about to get killed."

Esther became uneasy and fidgety and look at Matt.

"Jacob I think this is enough. I am worried about

your life, your safety" said Esther while hugging him and stroking his head.

"We have to go, this is not getting any better." Esther said further.

"Mom look, he's still alive." And he gestured Matt calmly.

"I know but this can endanger your life." And she looked at her son with much pity in her eyes.

The police arrived and they arrested the two men.

"How did you know all these?" Matt asked confusingly.

At first Elisha was silent then she looked at Jacob. She is not sure if Jacob wants her to tell her dad about these voices he is hearing.

"And why is this boy here?" Matt asked while very much puzzled.

"Dad, he's the reason why you are still alive. He saved your life."

"Him, how" He asked again still bewildered.

"You may not believe it, but he heard those two men talking, plotting to kill you but they will make it look like an accident."

Still Matt won't believe.

"He can hear now, isn't he deaf?"

"Yes he can hear only when bad things are about to happen to anybody."

"How did he hear those two men?"

"It's a long story dad."

"A long story.. you came all the way here to tell

me he heard two men plotting to kill me and it's a long story why a deaf boy could hear them."

"The good news is you're safe now." Elisha said assuredly.

When Esther heard Elisha talking she look at Jacob and asked whispering.

"How come she knows it, didn't I tell you not to let anybody know?"

"I'm sorry mom, she's my only friend and every time my ear vibrates I can't help but tell her and she's always been there for me when something happens, whenever I have to encounter some incidents. She is the only one I can bond with, and can count on no one else"

"Jacob ___ what have you been doing, why are you not telling me?"

"I have saved a little girl's life once, she was about to be hit by a big truck but I was able to help her avoid it and Elisha has been there for me."

He also told her mom that Elisha was with her during the robbery at the Jewelry store and how the robbers were caught by the police.

Esther was astounded to hear what Jacob had been doing.

Matt saw Jacob talking to his mother without using a sign language.

"Can he hear now?" Matt asked Elisha again.

"Not exactly dad, not just yet."

"Why is he not using a sign language?" Matt was confused again.

"He does not use a sign language only when he is involved in such a situation like this."

"What situation"

"In a situation when he is to get involve in saving lives."

Martha was astonished too upon hearing what Jacob can do.

"How come you did not tell us" Martha asked.

"I can't because I need to protect him." And looking at her dad she said.

"Do you remember that incident at the Toy Store, it was all over the News and on television for several days, where a suicidal man kidnapped a little girl inside the store and attempted to jump from the top of the building with her, Jacob and her mom were there too, he saved that little girl's life."

Esther decided to take Jacob home. "Let's go Jacob"

When Elisha saw them leaving she said.

"Jake, thanks!" And she waved her hand as a gesture of goodbye.

And Jacob nodded "Sure"

"So he can hear you now" Matt asked

"For now yes, after this moment not anymore."

Martha turned to Matt and asked curiously.

"Do you have any idea why those people wanted to kill you?"

"I can't think of any reason why."

"How about the way you deal with them, your treatment, have you been fair, understanding and patient in some ways?"

Matt couldn't answer.

Matt knew that he has been hard on those two men, for committing too much error in their work, he yelled and embarrassed them quite often and threatened to fire if they do not show improvement in their jobs.

When they reached home, Esther asked Jacob in sign language.

"Jake, can you stop going to Elisha at least for a while, please"

And he answered "Yes" in sign language just to appease her mom.

Despite all what's happening to Jacob, Esther has managed to maintain a solid mind level and stable attitude and tried to work at her best to support his son untiringly.

It is spring time warm and calm. Blue sky is cloudless, sun is bright but cool. Upon waking up one morning, Jacob went to his mother's garden to look at the flowers. The garden is rich with fresh blossoming spring flowers giving the air a lovely sweet smelling fragrance. The verdant lawn is lined with bed of white flowers bathed in brilliant sunlight producing a delightful and refreshing sight. The garden is alive with the sound of sweet singing birds.

Jacob unexpectedly noticed he can hear several sounds without his ear vibrating and without feeling any pain. He can hear the tweets and chirps of small birds, the sound of the wind whispering through the trees and the sound of the breeze as it sways the tiny stems and leaves of the flowers. At first he was so excited but he wants to test his hearing some more, he further went outside their gate and heard the neighbor's sound, the barking dogs and the sound of a starting engine of a vehicle.

"I can hear now?" He asked himself with astonishment.

With a smile on his face he went inside to tell her mom but he saw his two sisters watching cartoons on TV. For the first time with excitement and eagerness he wants to watch and listen to the dialogues. At first, the girls didn't notice Jacob, when they saw him watching for the first time Abigail asked in sign language.

"What are you doing here?"

"I just want to watch and listen." He answered using no sign language.

The two girls were surprised when they heard him talked and they look at each other when Jacob answered without using a sign language.

"Watch and listen?" Gracie asked astounded

"You mean you can hear now?" Abigail asked with amazement

"I think so." Jacob answered still not using a sign language.

Gracie rushed to see her mom

"Mom come Jake can hear now"

Esther thought Jacob is again hearing some voices somewhere else so she asked.

"What did he say where the voice or sound is coming from?"

"No mom, he can hear our conversation and he can watch the TV and listen to the sound"

"Huh..? what..?" Esther was stunned.

"Yes, he is there watching TV and can hear now."

"Jake is it true you can hear now?" Esther asked without using a sign language.

And Jacob answered with no sign language. "Yes mom."

"Did your ear vibrate, did you feel some pain?"

"No vibration and no pain mom" He answered.

"How did you experience hearing without vibration and pain?" Esther asked.

"I don't know it just happened I could hear every sound now."

Esther kissed and embraced Jacob tightly and said thankfully and cheerfully. "It's a miracle" "Thank you Lord."

In her excitement she called Luke to inform him about Jacob and Luke also became excited and said.

"I can't wait to go home"

When Luke came home his joy was indescribable, he at once hugged Jacob and talked to him using no sign language.

"I'm so happy for you my son how did you know you can hear now?"

"I went outside at the garden and heard all kinds

of sound there the leaves, the trees, the birds then I went out of the gate and heard the sounds of the neighbor even the barking dogs."

Esther and Luke look at each other smilingly. The two girls hugged him joyfully.

The following day, they went to the doctor and again he was asked to listen to the machine producing sounds of nature, and Jacob answered he can hear them all now. The doctor also played a CD from his own portable player and asked Jacob if he can hear the music, Jacob responded "Yes"

"This is amazing" the doctor said happily

Esther and her family were so happy at Jacob's improved condition and they went out to dinner to celebrate.

Jacob can now experience hearing the sound of the animals at the zoo, the sound of the gentle tiny waves lapping against the shore while his feet feeling the lukewarm clammy sand at the beach, the sound of the motorboats, jet skis, the seagulls' melodic cries, bird song in the morning, sound of musical instruments, and the cheering crowd at the soccer game where his father brought him for the first time.

When Elisha heard that Jacob gained his hearing she was so thrilled, happy and excited.

"So we will not use sign language anymore." Elisha said.

"I guess not anymore but not to be forgotten."

Matt saw Jacob and Elisha seated at the swing although reluctant he approached them and told Jacob.

"Jacob I think there is something I have almost forgotten to say, I want to apologize for being so rude, mean and intolerant in all these times. I didn't know one day you will save my life. And I haven't even thanked you yet, can you accept my apology and my thanks, I owe you my life."

"You're welcome Mr. Muirfield."

Elisha never felt so happy till he heard those words from her dad.

Jacob continues to hear sounds and voices from distant locations without feeling any vibration and pain from his ear. He continues to save lives and he goes to a regular school now attended by normal students. Jacob has yet to make some adjustment in his new classroom for the fifth graders. The classroom is noisy with mouthy children.

However once in a while he visits his former school for the deaf and was very sad to have left his classmates but happy that he does not go to that school anymore. It was a bittersweet goodbye for Jacob. That morning he stopped by, a flow of excitement run through the classroom, his classmates missed him but are happy for him now that he can hear normally.

When Angeline saw him once more there was a big smile and glow on her face but with a feeling of sadness when she talked to him.

"Maybe we may not be seeing you often anymore Jacob, you are now in the bright world."

Jacob was touched at what Angeline expressed in sign language and he answered.

"You don't have to put it that way Angeline. We all live in the bright world. My mom has always told me to look at the bright side no matter how bleak it is, for there is always light."

When Angeline sees Jacob conveys to her those words she felt good.

"I'm just too happy for you Jacob, but I felt losing a friend."Now she is talking while using sign language.

"You have not lost me Angeline, I'm still here."

"But you are not one of us anymore."

"Nothing has changed I'll try to come and visit every so often I can, I also missed this place, life is so quiet and peaceful here."

Before it's time for him to say goodbye, he said to Angeline.

"Always have that hope thriving in your heart. God has always a way for all His children."

Jacob has noticed some progress in Angeline's voice she speaks with a little clarity in her words, less slurred with reduced difficulty and not slow anymore.

"Do you still go to your speech therapist?"

"Yes"

"Keep it up. I think you're doing all right. I noticed you're improving."

"Thank you."

"Take care of yourself Angel and always stay happy, okay."

"You too Jacob"

"Bye, now."

As Jacob left the classroom Angeline had mixed emotions. She was sad Jacob can no longer be in their class, glad for Jacob's normal condition, and with Jacob's inspiring live through experience she wished someday she too could enjoy the sound of the world before long.

Sometimes Jacob volunteers to be the sign language interpreter whenever there are some occasions for celebrating in the community where there is a need to use a sign language.

He was also being invited to give speeches to group of hearing impaired children also being attended by normal children interested to hear him talk and with the aid of a sign language interpreter he delivers powerful speeches on encouragement reflect on hope and on what God can do in moments when humans are incapable of doing something.

"Whatever your handicap is, don't disregard or discount yourself, don't look at it as a disadvantage

but a blessing, for you never know what you have inside and what God has in store for you." He said in one of his speeches.

One day Elisha and Jacob were at their garden, by force of habit she used a sign language to communicate with him.

"Oh I'm sorry I shouldn't be using this anymore." She said smilingly.

Jacob just smiled and said. "It's okay let's just say we don't want to totally forget this sign language that brought us closer together." Jacob said and they hugged each other.

His encounter to save other people's lives has become lesser and fewer to the point that he does not do it anymore he now lives the normal and ordinary life of a boy, still goes to the crucifix garden and continues to offer flowers and prayers. Once more he closed his eyes and said.

"Lord, thank you for this lifetime special gift you have given me, whatever it is that I cannot do anymore, I'll leave it all into your hands, please do it all for me."

THE END

Printed in the United States
By Bookmasters